Rafi and Rosi Music!

Lulu Delacre

Children's Book Press, *an imprint of* Lee & Low Books Inc.
New York

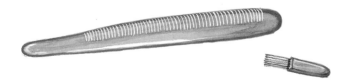

Not even the fiercest hurricane can do away with the music of Puerto Rico!

Acknowledgments

I'm grateful to Dr. Ángel G. Quintero Rivera, Centro de Investigaciones Sociales, University of Puerto Rico, for reviewing the informational material in the "Did You Know About . . ." section of the book; and Ángel Rivera, director of Cultura Plenera, who also reviewed the "Did You Know About . . ." section and created his own version of the musical notation for the song *"Temporal, temporal." Gracias* to Josarie Molina and Garwin Zamora, Puerto Rican educators at DC Bilingual Public Charter School, Washington, DC, and to members of the ensemble Los Hijo 'e Plena for reviewing the stories. *Gracias* to Julia L. Gutiérrez-Rivera of the ensemble Los Pleneros de la 21 for answering my questions about *bomba* dance and rhythm. *Gracias* to Manuel Hernández, music teacher at DC Bilingual Public Charter School, for his help with Rosie's rap. Thank you also to Louise May for her incredibly careful editing.

"Bámbula eh sea allá" is a traditional *bomba* song in the public domain. The writer is unknown. Some experts credit *"Temporal, temporal"* to Juan Barquet, circa 1920. Other experts credit the song to Rafael Hernández, who composed a version after the San Felipe Segundo (Okeechobee) hurricane hit Puerto Rico in 1928. The excerpted lyrics from the song that appear on pages 32 and 35 were incorporated into the original *plena* tune by Tony Croatto in the 1970s.

Author's Sources

Álvarez, Luis Manuel y Ángel G. Quintero Rivera. "Bambulaé sea allá: la bomba y la plena. Compendio histórico-social". http://musica.uprrp.
    edu/lalvarez/bambulae_sea_%20alla_files/bomba_plena.html.
Echevarría Alvarado, Félix. *La Plena: Origen, Sentido y Desarrollo en el Folklore Puertorriqueño*. Bloomington, IN: Indiana University
    Press, 1984.
Guadalupe Pérez, Hiram. "Breve historia de la salsa." Enciclopedia de Puerto Rico, September 11, 2014. Spanish: https://enciclopediapr.org/
    encyclopedia/breve-historia-de-la-salsa/; English: https://enciclopediapr.org/en/encyclopedia/brief-history-of-salsa-music/.
Joglar, Rafael L. *Los Coquíes de Puerto Rico: Su historia natural y conservación*. San Juan: Editorial de la Universidad de Puerto Rico, 1998.
López Cruz, Francisco. *La música folklórica de Puerto Rico*. Sharon, CT: Troutman Press, 1967.
Malavet Vega, Pedro. *La plena que yo conozco*. Santo Domingo, Dominican Republic: Editora Corripio, 2001.
"Puerto Rican *Bomba* and *Plena*: Shared Traditions—Distinct Rhythms." Smithsonian Folkways Recordings. https://folkways.si.edu/puerto-
    rican-bomba-plena-shared-traditions-distinct-rhythms/latin-world/music/article/smithsonian.
"Puerto Rico (Bomba y Plena)." Islas de Borinken TV Documentary, March 3, 2013. https://m.youtube.com/watch?t=708s&v=mvTX6YA30Lc.
"Salsa." Music of Puerto Rico. http://www.musicofpuertorico.com/index.php/genre/salsa/.

Edited by Louise E. May • Designed by David and Susan Neuhaus/NeuStudio
Production by The Kids at Our House
The text is set in Times Regular
The illustrations are rendered in watercolor and colored pencil on Arches watercolor paper
Manufactured in China by Imago • Printed on paper from responsible sources
(HC) 10 9 8 7 6 5 4 3 2 1
(PBK) 10 9 8 7 6 5 4 3
First Edition
Library of Congress Cataloging-in-Publication Data
Names: Delacre, Lulu, author illustrator.
Title: Rafi and Rosi : music! / Lulu Delacre. Other titles: Music!
Description: First edition. | New York : Children's Book Press, an imprint of Lee & Low Books Inc., [2019] |
Series: Dive into reading! | Summary: "Rafi and Rosi, two curious tree frogs, explore the bomba, plena, and
salsa music traditions of their home island, Puerto Rico" — Provided by publisher. | Includes bibliographical references.
Identifiers: LCCN 2018044280 | ISBN 9780892394296 (hardcover : alk. paper) | ISBN 9780892394319 (pbk. : alk. paper)
Subjects: | CYAC: Tree frogs—Fiction. | Frogs—Fiction. | Brothers and sisters—Fiction. | Music—Puerto Rico—Fiction. |
Dance—Puerto Rico—Fiction. | Puerto Rico—Fiction.
Classification: LCC PZ7.D3696 Rcm 2019 | DDC [E]—dc23
LC record available at https://lccn.loc.gov/2018044280

Contents

Glossary

¡A bailar! (ah bye-LAR): Go dance!

¡Ay, bendito! (EYE ben-DEE-toh): Oh dear!

barril (bah-RREEL): Barrel; in *bomba*: drum.

batey (bah-TEHY): Gathering place.

bomba (BOHM-bah): Musical style; also a drum, dance, and/or song.

¡Chévere! (CHEH-veh-reh): Great!

coquí (koh-KEE): Tiny tree frog found in Puerto Rico that is named after its song.

cuento (KUHEHN-toh): Story.

fiesta de barrio (fee-EHS-tah deh BAH-rreeoh): Neighborhood party.

gracias (GRAH-seeahs): Thank you.

güiro (guh-EEH-roh): Gourd instrument.

lindo (LIN-doh): Nice, pretty.

Loíza (lo-EEH-sah): Town on the northeastern coast of Puerto Rico.

maraca (mah-RAH-cah): Rattle.

¡Me pica! (meh PEE-cah): It itches!

paella (pah-EH-yah): Rice and seafood dish.

pandero (pahn-DEH-roh): Shallow drum.

> **punteador (puhn-teh-ah-DOHR):** Lowest-pitched drum.
>
> **requinto: (reh-KEEN-toh):** Higher-pitched drum.
>
> **seguidor: (seh-guee-DOHR):** Highest-pitched drum.

plena (PLEH-nah): Musical style; also a song.

primo (PREE-moh): In music, a lead instrument.

salsa (SAHL-sah): Musical style; also means "sauce."

Santurce (sahn-TUHR-ceh): District of San Juan, Puerto Rico.

¡Seguro! (seh-GUH-roh): Sure! Of course!

¡Sí! (SEE): Yes!

surullito (suh-ruh-YEE-toh): Corn fritter.

viste (VEEHS-teh): See.

Fiery Bomba

"*Sea, sea, sea allá,*

bámbula eh sea allá . . ."

the crowd sang

to the throbbing beat

of the *bomba* drums.

6

Rafi and Rosi Coquí were in Loíza

with Rafi's music teacher, Don Toño.

Rosi felt squeezed out

by the big, tall crowd.

She stretched her neck.

"I can't see," she said to Rafi,

her older brother.

"Let's climb up
this mango tree,"
said Rafi.
"*¡Sí!*" agreed Rosi.
"Yes!"

Perched on a thick branch,
Rosi and Rafi could see
all the action in the *batey*,
the place for *bomba*
drums, dance, and song.

8

Bomba drummers tap-tapped
their *barriles*,
their tall *bomba* drums.
Then the lead singer
broke into song—
call-and-answer, call-and-answer—
and the crowd sang along.
Soon a dancer strolled
into the center of the *batey*
and bowed to the *primo*,
the lead drum.

Big beats boomed, big beats thundered,

and a red *maraca* rattled.

Rosi noticed that one drummer's

tap-tapping was not like the others.

"He isn't following along!" she said.

"He's playing the *primo*," said Rafi.

"His beats match the dancer's moves."

"What do you mean?" asked Rosi.

"*Bomba* dance is a back-and-forth between the dancer and drummer. He plays some cool beats on the *primo*. Then the dancer challenges the drummer to create more beats that follow her moves," said Rafi.

"I see," said Rosi.

The tree was heavy with sweet fruit.

Rafi picked two ripe mangoes.

"Here," he said, giving one to Rosi.

"*Gracias*," said Rosi, her eyes glued

to the scene below. "Thank you."

"Watch that dancer!" exclaimed Rafi.

The dancer swished her skirt

left and right, right and left.

Drumbeats rolled, drumbeats rippled.

Big booming beats rumbled

after each swirl and shake.

"It's amazing!" Rosi exclaimed,

bouncing up and down.

She imagined she was the dancer

making music with her own moves.

"I wish I could try those drums,"

Rafi said, tapping his fingers.

14

Suddenly the *bomba* singer called
all young dancers and drummers
to come and try their skills.
Rosi dropped her half-eaten mango
and turned to look at Rafi.
Neither of them could wait.

15

"*Bomba* drums, here I come!"

hollered Rafi.

One big jump

and he was on his way.

Rosi jumped too,

squashing the juicy mango

as she landed.

She ran all the way to the *batey*.

Rosi wanted to make music

with her moves!

At the edge of the crowd

she stood on a big mound of dirt

so the singer could see her.

But the mound wasn't just dirt.

The mound was a fire ant hill.

"¡A bailar!" called
the singer. "Go dance!"
Rosi hopped into the circle.
First she bowed
to the *primo* drum.
Then she swished her arms
left and right, right and left.
Drumbeats rolled . . .
drumbeats rippled.
Big booming beats rumbled
after each swirl and shake.

"Bravo, Rosi!" Rafi shouted.
But suddenly Rosi started
to jump and shake
and swipe and slap
in a frenzied *bomba* dance.
Drumbeats rolled . . .
drumbeats rippled.
Big booming beats
bellowed faster and faster,
but they could not keep up
with Rosi's dancing.

Rafi was puzzled.

So was the crowd.

"*¡Me pica, me pica!*" Rosi burst out.

"It itches! It itches!"

"Look," said someone in the crowd.

"Ants are biting her!"

So the singer made this up:

"*Pica aquí, pica allá,*

bámbula eh sea allá.

Fiery bomba pa' gozar,

bámbula eh sea allá . . ."

Rosi saw froggies pointing at her,

and she heard froggies giggling.

She covered her ears

and ran from the *batey* to hide

behind the mango tree.

She began to cry.

Rafi ran after her.

"Are you okay?" Rafi asked.

"No!" Rosi yelled.

"They made fun of me."

"Well, not really," Rafi said.

Rosi sniffled.

Rafi put his arm around her.

"It's a tradition to make up songs
about what happens in the *batey*."

Rosi looked up.

"You're famous now," added Rafi.

"You think so?" Rosi asked.

"*¡Seguro!*" exclaimed Rafi. "Sure!

They've made up

a *bomba* song

just for you!"

Rosi wiped away

her tears.

"Yes," she said.

"They did."

She gave Rafi a hug.

Rafi and Rosi raced back
to the *batey* singing,
"Pica aquí, pica allá,
bámbula eh sea allá.

Fiery bomba pa' gozar,
bámbula eh sea allá . . ."

"Finished!" said Rafi.

He was pleased with his *güiro*.

He had spent weeks

making the instrument.

Don Toño had shown him how.

First Rafi chose
a long gourd
and hung it up to dry.

When the gourd was dry,
he scrubbed it clean.

Then Rafi carved
narrow notches
along one side
of the gourd.

Rosi was making paper flowers

on the porch of their home in Santurce.

"Isn't my *güiro* cool?" Rafi asked Rosi.

"*Lindo*," Rosi said. "Nice."

"I'll use it to earn money to buy Mamá

a necklace for Mother's Day," said Rafi.

"How?" asked Rosi.

"By playing *plena* songs on the street,"
said Rafi.

Rafi picked up the metal tool

to play his *güiro*

and headed toward the front gate.

"Wait!" said Rosi.

"I'm going with you!"

"No, you're not," said Rafi.

"Big brothers only."

And then he was gone.

Rosi frowned,

and pouted,

and thought.

She stuffed

her paper flowers

into her tin,

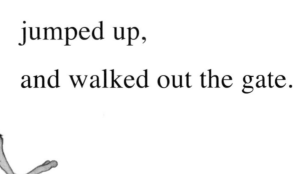

jumped up,

and walked out the gate.

31

Rafi stood alone at the corner.

He had set out a can for coins.

"*Temporal, temporal,*

allá viene el temporal . . ."

he sang to the scrape-scraping rhythm

of his *güiro*—

down-up-up, down-up-up.

Rosi marched over

and planted herself in front of

Don Toño's music store.

She began to string

her paper flowers into a crown.

Now and then she peeked at Rafi,

the frown still on her face.

As time went by,
Rosi noticed
that no one stopped
to listen to Rafi.
No one dropped coins
in his can.

Rafi looked a bit sad.
Little by little
Rosi's frown lifted.
She put on the crown
of paper flowers and
walked over to Rafi.

34

"Can I sing with you?" Rosi asked.

Rafi shrugged. "Okay," he said.

Rosi jumped onto a doorstep.

She held her tin like a *pandero*,

the short, handheld *plena* drum.

She tap-tapped as they sang,

"*Temporal, temporal,*

allá viene el temporal . . ."

One of Don Toño's customers saw
Rosi join Rafi to sing *plena* songs.
He called to everyone in the store.
Don Toño came out tap-tapping
his *seguidor pandero* drum.
He set a rhythm, a steady rumble
of beats that wouldn't change—
same beats, same; same beats, same.

Then a froggie came
pounding a smaller drum,
a *punteador pandero*,
and stressing just some beats—
drumbeats rolling over drumbeats.
Another froggie rapped
a *requinto pandero* drum—
making up high-pitched beats
and rounding out the *plena* party
that spilled onto the street.

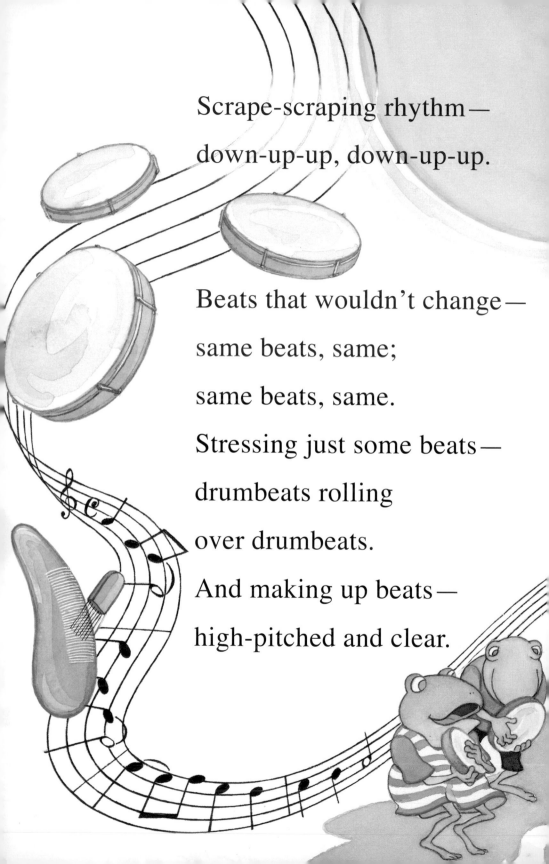

Scrape-scraping rhythm—
down-up-up, down-up-up.

Beats that wouldn't change—
same beats, same;
same beats, same.
Stressing just some beats—
drumbeats rolling
over drumbeats.
And making up beats—
high-pitched and clear.

The crowd swelled with joy
on this sunny
playing-singing-dancing
plena music day.
Rosi picked up Rafi's
can and danced her way
around the froggies
until the crowd
trickled away.

"Good *güiro*," said Don Toño

before leaving. "Well played."

"*Gracias*," said Rafi. "Thank you."

Rosi came over to Rafi

and handed him his can.

"Rosi, it's full!"
Rafi exclaimed.
"*¿Viste?*" Rosi said.
"See! Little sisters
can help."

Rafi handed Rosi his *güiro*.
Then he lifted up
his little sister
and carried her
on his shoulders
all the way
to the gift shop.

At the store Rafi and Rosi

shopped around and found

the perfect necklace for Mamá.

And they did it together.

Hot
Salsa

"*¡Chévere!*" said Rafi. "Great!"

He burst into Rosi's room

flashing an invitation.

"What?" asked Rosi.

She had been listening to their

neighbor's rap music all day.

"Don Toño is having his *fiesta de barrio* tonight," Rafi said. "Everyone comes to the neighborhood party and plays instruments. Let me get my *güiro*!"

"I'll get ready," Rosi said. She went to look for something sparkly to wear.

45

The sun was low in the sky
when Rafi and Rosi left.
On their way to Don Toño's
Rafi began to hum.
"What's that song?"
asked Rosi.

"A *salsa*," said Rafi.

"It's called '*Che Che Colé*,'
and it's by two famous musicians."

"*¿Salsa?*" Rosi said.

"Sauce? How did it
get that name?"

Rafi smiled a sneaky smile
and began his tall tale.
"Long ago two musicians,
Héctor and Willie,
were sharing their new sound
with a friend at lunch,"
Rafi said. "They bragged
that the music featured
a chorus,
a lead singer,
and nine instruments."

"The friend asked the musicians

the name of their new sound,"

Rafi continued.

"Héctor and Willie shrugged.

Just then a waitress tripped

and dropped a bowl of sauce on them.

'*¡La salsa!*' the musicians screamed.

And that's how their sound

got its name."

"Wow," Rosi said. "You know a lot!"

"Yeah," said Rafi.

As they rounded a corner,
the spicy sounds spilling from
Don Toño's house
bubbled and popped.
Inside, loud chatter blended
with the sounds of *conga* drums,
maracas, and horns.
Outside on the patio young and old
were *salsa*-dancing.

From deep within the kitchen
the mouth-watering aroma of *paella*,
rice topped with mussels and shrimp,
reached Rosi.

She stepped inside.

"Rosi!" said her friend Tita.

"Here. Have a *surullito*.

The corn fritters are still hot."

Rosi dipped a warm fritter
into its garlicky pink sauce.
She remembered Rafi's story.

"I know why they call it *salsa*,"
said Rosi, pointing to the dancers.
"Really?" Tita said. "Why?"

"Long ago . . . ," Rosi started.

Many froggies leaned in to listen.

Don Toño was there too.

". . . and they screamed, '*¡La salsa!*'

That's how the musicians' new sound

got its name!" Rosi finished.

Rafi saw Don Toño's frown,

and he tried to run away.

"Rosi," said Don Toño gently.

"That's not a true story."

"But Rafi told it to me!"

Rosi cried, her cheeks burning.

Rafi had tricked her.

Again.

Angry words came to Rosi.

She climbed onto a stool,

looking for Rafi.

"Rafi!" called Rosi.

She started rapping.

Why you tell me stuff
  that is not true?
You tell it so, and I trust you.

Dumb, dumb cuentos
  make me mad.
Some of your stories
  make me look bad.
I don't want untrue stuff
  No. No more.
I don't want to hear you, I roar!

The crowd fell silent.

The music stopped.

Rosi jumped down from the stool.

Rafi walked up to her.

He hadn't meant to upset her.

"*¡Ay bendito!*" Rafi sighed.

"Sorry for the story," he said.

"But . . . it could be true."

"How?" asked Rosi.

"*Salsa* has *bomba*, *plena*, and a bunch of other rhythms all mixed in — like a sauce," Rafi said.

"He's right," agreed Don Toño.

The music started again.

"Want to dance?" Rafi asked Rosi.

"Hmm . . . ," she said. "Let me think."

"*¡Sí!*" Rosi yelled. "Yes!"

And Rafi and Rosi *salsa*-danced

until their feet hurt

and the sky

was sprinkled with stars.

Did You Know About . . .

. . . *Bomba?*

Bomba is three things: a drum, a dance, and a song. This musical style dates back to the early 1700s and is an important foundation of Puerto Rican music. *Bomba* emerged from the musical traditions of enslaved Africans in Spanish-occupied Puerto Rico. The music evolved as these enslaved people interacted with other enslaved Africans on neighboring Caribbean islands. This resulted in at least sixteen different *bomba* rhythms.

Bombaa is a word that means "drum" in Ashanti, a West African dialect. In Puerto Rico, the word became *bomba*. *Bomba* drums are also called *barriles* because the drums were originally made out of discarded wood barrels. *Bomba* instruments include *barriles* that can be tuned to be played as a *primo*, high-pitched drum, or a *buleador*, low-pitched drum; a *maraca*; and sticks called *cuás* that are commonly banged on the side of a small drum. *Buleador* drums keep a basic rhythm that remains constant, while the *primo*, or lead, drum improvises beats in a fluid conversation with the dancer.

In the current Puerto Rican tradition of *bomba*, a dancer strolls into the *batey*, a gathering place, surrounded by a crowd and musicians. After bowing to the *primo* drum, a dialogue begins between the dancer and the *primo* drummer. The drummer creates beats to catch the dancer's attention, and the dancer challenges the drummer to follow her or his movements.

Usually *bomba* events are communal. A singer leads the crowd in a well-known *bomba* song, such as "*Bámbula eh sea allá*," and the crowd becomes the chorus in a call-and-response fashion. The singer may add improvised verses to the original lyrics to reflect what goes on in the *batey* at the moment.

61

. . . Plena?

Plena dates to the early 1900s. It originated in coastal towns, where most of the Afro-Puerto Rican population lived. *Plena* shares *bomba*'s call-and-response singing tradition and use of percussion instruments.

Plena's percussion instruments are small and easy to carry. Workers moving from sugarcane fields to factories would travel with them. The instruments include shallow, handheld drums, called *panderos*, and a *güiro*, a notched gourd. The *güiro* dates back to the native Taínos living in Puerto Rico in the 1400s. Sometimes other instruments, such as a guitar or a harmonica, are also used to support the melody of a song.

Today, three *panderos* of different sizes and tones are usual. The *seguidor pandero* establishes the basic rhythm and tempo of a song. The *punteador pandero* layers on beats that accent the *seguidor*'s unstressed beats. The *requinto pandero* improvises, adding flourishes to the rhythm. The *güiro* always follows the *seguidor pandero*'s rhythm and tempo. *Plena* has only one rhythm, which varies in tempo according to the lyrics of each song.

Plena is known as the people's sung newspaper. Since the beginning, the focus has always been on the story a *plena* song narrates. "*Temporal, temporal*" is a *plena* song that many experts credit to Rafael Hernández. It tells of a fierce hurricane on its way to Puerto Rico in 1928. Many groups in Puerto Rico use *plena* rhythm for political slogans and songs of protest.

People usually dance *plena* as couples, a custom brought by the Spanish. Although dance is not integral to the *plena* musical tradition, group-dancing to live music has become common in recent decades. Puerto Ricans sing and play *plena* at festivals, holidays, and spontaneous street gatherings called *plenazos*.

62

. . . How to Make a *Güiro*?

Be sure to ask an adult to help you make a traditional Puerto Rican güiro.

You will need: a long, dried gourd*; sink filled with warm water; scrubbing pad; towel; masking tape; pencil; serrated knife; permanent markers (optional); metal comb or hair pik.

1) Soak the gourd in water for 15 minutes.
2) Using the scrubbing pad, remove the outer skin of the gourd so that the golden inner skin shows.
3) Place the gourd on the towel on a flat surface.
4) Put two strips of masking tape along the length of the gourd, 1½" to 3" apart, depending on the width of the gourd. These are the guides for the sides of the *güiro*'s ridges.
5) With the pencil, draw parallel lines very close together across the gourd between the tape guides.
6) Hold the gourd firmly. Using the serrated knife, go back and forth over each pencil line to carve ridges in the gourd.
7) If you wish, use the markers to decorate the smooth side of the gourd.

When the gourd is finished, scrape the comb or hair pik up and down over the ridges of the *güiro* to make music!

Gourds are available at farmer's markets, in some supermarkets, and online.

. . . Salsa?

There is no agreement about the origin of the name *salsa* for the hot, urban form of music that has spread worldwide. But experts do agree that the musical style we know as *salsa* began to be called by that name during the 1960s.

Puerto Ricans who migrated to New York City in the 1950s established themselves in the city's poorer neighborhoods. Often they found themselves unwelcome. Looking for a sense of belonging, they gathered with other Latinx/Caribbean immigrants. A common heritage among these migrants was music rooted in African rhythms.

Puerto Rican musicians in New York began harmonizing Latin rhythms such as *bomba*, *plena*, and Cuban *son montuno, guaracha,* and *samba*. They usually added African American sounds, including jazz, rhythm and blues, and soul, and alternated these sounds with the Puerto Rican rhythmic pattern called *clave*. The result was rich music that made people want to both listen and get up and dance.

Salsa music may include percussion, wind, and string instruments. Bongos, conga drums, timbals (kettledrums), *maracas*, *güiros*, claves (thick, wooden sticks), cowbells, horns, violins, guitars, and a piano are commonly used. There is also a chorus and a soloist. As in *bomba* and *plena*, the call-and-response song tradition and the element of improvisation are present in *salsa*.

Today, *salsa* boasts many talented vocalists and composers. Among the earliest were Héctor Lavoe and Willie Colón. They met in New York City, and in 1969 released *Cosa Nuestra*, a Gold record album on which the *salsa* song "*Che Che Colé*" appears.

. . . the Songs Rafi and Rosi Sing?

BÁMBULA EH SEA ALLÁ
Sea, sea, sea allá, (SEH-ah, SEH-ah, SEH-ah ah-LLA):
    Right there, just there,
bámbula eh sea allá . . . (BAHM-buh-lah eh SEH-ah ah-LLA):
    it is there where we remember. . .
Pica aquí, pica allá, (PEE-cah ah-KEE, PEE-cah ah-LLA):
    It itches here, it itches there,
bámbula eh sea allá. (BAHM-buh-lah eh SEH-ah ah-LLA):
    it is there where we remember.
Fiery bomba pa' gozar, (FAHYUH-ree BOHM-bah pah goh-ZAHR):
    Fiery bomba to enjoy,
bámbula eh sea allá . . . (BAHM-buh-lah eh SEH-ah ah-LLA):
    it is there where we remember . . .

TEMPORAL, TEMPORAL
Temporal, temporal, (tehm-poh-RAHL, tehm-poh-RAHL):
    Hurricane, hurricane,
allá viene el temporal . . . (ah-LLA vee-EH-neh ehl tehm-poh-RAHL):
    there comes the hurricane . . .